DK READERS

Level 2

Dinosaur Dinners
Fire Fighter!
Bugs! Bugs! Bugs!
Slinky, Scaly Snakes!
Animal Hospital
The Little Ballerina
Munching, Crunching, Sniffing,
    and Snooping
The Secret Life of Trees
Winking, Blinking, Wiggling,
    and Waggling
Astronaut: Living in Space
Twisters!
Holiday! Celebration Days
    around the World
The Story of Pocahontas
Horse Show
Survivors: The Night the Titanic Sank
Eruption! The Story of Volcanoes
The Story of Columbus
Journey of a Humpback Whale
Amazing Buildings
Feathers, Flippers, and Feet
Outback Adventure: Australian Holiday
Sniffles, Sneezes, Hiccups, and Coughs

Let's Go Riding
Starry Sky
Earth Smart: How to Take Care
    of the Environment
Water Everywhere
Telling Time
A Trip to the Theatre
Journey of a Pioneer
Star Wars: Journey Through Space
Star Wars: A Queen's Diary
Star Wars: R2-D2 and Friends
Star Wars: Jedi in Training
Star Wars: Join the Rebels
Star Wars The Clone Wars: Anakin in
    Action!
Star Wars The Clone Wars: Stand
    Aside – Bounty Hunters!
Spider-Man: Worst Enemies
Power Rangers: Great Adventures
Pokémon: Meet the Pokémon
Pokémon: Meet Ash!
Indiana Jones: Traps and Snares
Meet the X-Men

Level 3

Shark Attack!
Beastly Tales
Titanic
Invaders from Outer Space
Movie Magic
Time Traveller
Bermuda Triangle
Tiger Tales
Plants Bite Back!
Zeppelin: The Age of the Airship
Spies
Terror on the Amazon
Disasters at Sea
The Story of Anne Frank
Extreme Sports
Spiders' Secrets
The Big Dinosaur Dig
The Story of Chocolate
School Days Around the World
Welcome to China
My First Ballet Show
Ape Adventures

Greek Myths
Star Wars: Star Pilot
Star Wars: I Want to Be a Jedi
Star Wars: The Story of Darth Vader
Star Wars: Yoda in Action
Star Wars: Forces of Darkness
Star Wars: Death Star Battles
Star Wars: Feel the Force
Star Wars The Clone Wars: Forces of
    Darkness
Star Wars The Clone Wars: Yoda in
    Action!
Star Wars The Clone Wars: Jedi Heroes
Marvel Heroes: Amazing Powers
The X-Men School
The Invincible Iron Man: Friends and
    Enemies
Wolverine: Awesome Powers
Fantastic Four: The World's Greatest
    Superteam
Fantastic Four: Adversaries

A Note to Parents

DK READERS is a compelling program for beginning readers, designed in conjunction with leading literacy experts, including Dr. Linda Gambrell, Professor of Education at Clemson University. Dr. Gambrell has served as President of the National Reading Conference and the College Reading Association, and has recently been elected to serve as President of the International Reading Association.

Beautiful illustrations and superb full-color photographs combine with engaging, easy-to-read stories to offer a fresh approach to each subject in the series. Each DK READER is guaranteed to capture a child's interest while developing his or her reading skills, general knowledge, and love of reading.

The five levels of DK READERS are aimed at different reading abilities, enabling you to choose the books that are exactly right for your child:

Pre-level 1: Learning to read
Level 1: Beginning to read
Level 2: Beginning to read alone
Level 3: Reading alone
Level 4: Proficient readers

The "normal" age at which a child begins to read can be anywhere from three to eight years old. Adult participation through the lower levels is very helpful for providing encouragement, discussing storylines, and sounding out unfamiliar words.

No matter which level you select, you can be sure that you are helping your child learn to read, then read to learn!

LONDON, NEW YORK, MUNICH,
MELBOURNE, AND DELHI

For Dorling Kindersley
Senior Editor Elizabeth Dowsett
Managing Art Editor Ron Stobbart
Managing Editor Catherine Saunders
Brand Manager Lisa Lanzarini
Publishing Manager Simon Beecroft
Category Publisher Alex Allan
Production Editor Siu Yin Chan
Production Controller Rita Sinha
Reading Consultant Dr. Linda Gambrell

For Lucasfilm
Executive Editor J. W. Rinzler
Art Director Troy Alders
Keeper of the Holocron Leland Chee
Director of Publishing Carol Roeder

Designed and edited by Tall Tree Ltd
Designer Ben Ruocco
Editor Jon Richards

First published in the United States in 2010
by DK Publishing
375 Hudson Street, New York, New York 10014

10 11 12 13 14 10 9 8 7 6 5 4 3 2 1

DK books are available at special discounts when purchased in bulk
for sales promotions, premiums, fund-raising, or educational use.
For details, contact: DK Publishing Special Markets
375 Hudson Street, New York, New York 10014
SpecialSales@dk.com

A catalog record for this book is available
from the Library of Congress.

ISBN: 978-0-7566-6880-8 (Hardback)
ISBN: 978-0-7566-6691-0 (Paperback)

Reproduced by Media Development and Printing Ltd., UK
Printed and bound in the United States by
Lake Book Manufacturing, Inc.

Discover more at:
www.dk.com
www.starwars.com

Contents

4   Clone army

6   Kamino

8   Jango Fett

10 Into battle

12 Clone armor

14 Speeder bikes

16 Clone pilot

18 Clones turn bad

20 Stormtroopers

22 Special troopers

24 Hunting Rebels

26 In disguise

28 Death Star

30 Victory!

32 Quiz

DK READERS

STAR WARS
CLONE TROOPERS
IN ACTION

Clare Hibbert

What a huge army! These soldiers are clone troopers. Every soldier is the same. The soldiers are human, but they wear armor that makes them look like robots.

The troopers fight
for the Republic.
So do the Jedi.

The Jedi
The Jedi are warriors
who fight for good.
Not all of the Jedi are
human. They are many
different creatures.

Obi-Wan Kenobi was the first
Jedi to see the clone troopers.
He discovered the army on a
planet near the edge of the galaxy.
This planet is called Kamino.

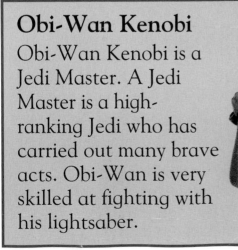

Obi-Wan Kenobi

Obi-Wan Kenobi is a
Jedi Master. A Jedi
Master is a high-
ranking Jedi who has
carried out many brave
acts. Obi-Wan is very
skilled at fighting with
his lightsaber.

This is Jango
Fett. He is very
good at fighting.
All the clone
troopers are
copies of Jango. Scientists made
the clone babies and grew them
inside glass jars. The babies will
grow into troopers.

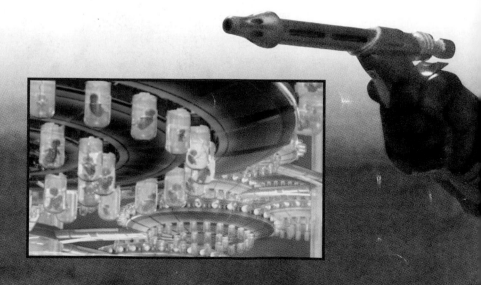

Clones

Clones are exact copies of living things.
Thousands of clones of Jango Fett have been
made to create the clone army.

The clones are off to fight their first battle. They fly to the battle inside huge warships. Jedi Master Yoda flies with them. He is a very wise Jedi. He is hundreds of years old.

The clone troopers wear helmets
and tough body armor. The armor
covers the troopers' bodies.

The armor is very strong
so that it protects the
clone troopers in battle.

Officers

Clone officers wear blue, green, red, or yellow stripes on their armor. Yellow is for the highest rank— clone commander.

Zoom! These clone troopers are driving speeder bikes. The bikes fly high above the ground.

They are super-fast and are used
to soar above a planet's surface.
The bikes have blaster cannons
to fire at enemies.

This is an even faster way to travel! This starfighter is flown by a clone pilot. Starfighters are small and fast ships. They are often launched from larger ships to attack the enemy.

Clone pilots

Just like the clone troopers, clone pilots are exact copies of Jango Fett.

Oh no! These clone troopers are attacking a Jedi. What is going on? Chancellor Palpatine has told everyone that the Jedi are bad. He orders the clone troopers to attack the Jedi suddenly so that the Jedi can't fight back.

Evil leader

Chancellor Palpatine is hungry for power. He pretends to be good, but he will stop at nothing to take control of the whole galaxy.

Now the troopers are called
stormtroopers. They don't fight with
the Jedi. They fight against them.
The stormtroopers obey Palpatine
and his second-in-command, Darth
Vader. Palpatine is now called the
Emperor and he rules the galaxy.

Darth Vader

Darth Vader
is part-human
and part-machine.
He was once a Jedi
Knight called Anakin
Skywalker, but now he
has turned to evil.

Some stormtroopers have special jobs. Scout troopers check out enemy territory. Snowtroopers fight on icy worlds. No matter what their job, all stormtroopers are well known for one thing—they always follow orders!

*Scout
trooper*

Snowtrooper

This tall walking tank is called an AT-AT. It carries stormtroopers into battle.
They are looking for Princess Leia and the secret Rebel base on an icy planet called Hoth.
Quick! Stop those walkers!

Rebels
The Rebel Alliance is fighting against Emperor Palpatine and the stormtroopers. Princess Leia is one of the Rebel commanders.

Stormtroopers are strong, but they are no match for Chewbacca. Get them, Chewie! Wait! These aren't stormtroopers!

Luke and his friend Han Solo are wearing stormtrooper armor as a disguise!

These stormtroopers are on a very large spaceship called the Death Star. They are guarding the Death Star from any Rebel attacks.

Death Star
The Death Star is shaped like an enormous ball. It is powerful enough to destroy an entire planet!

Can Luke, Han, and Leia defeat the stormtroopers and destroy the Death Star?

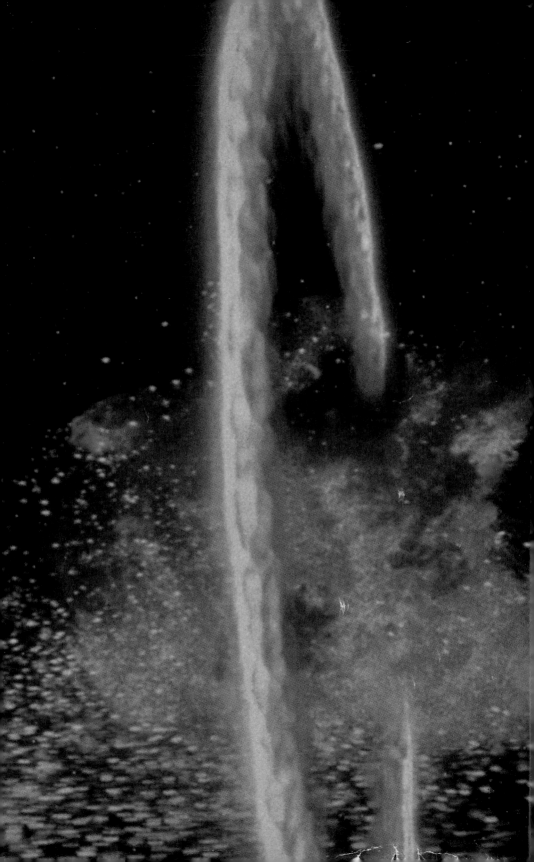

But what will happen to the
stormtroopers?
Will they rise again to fight
the valiant Rebels?

Quiz

1. Are clone troopers robots?

2. Who was cloned to make the troopers?

3. Where were the first clone troopers from?

4. What rank is this yellow clone trooper?

5. Who is this Rebel commander ?

6. Who gives orders to the stormtroopers?

Answers: 1. No, they are humans. 2. Jango Fett, a bounty hunter. 3. The planet Kamino. 4. Commander. 5. Princess Leia. 6. Darth Vader and Palpatine.

Index

armor 12, 27
AT-AT 24
Chewbacca 26
clone pilots 17
clones 8, 9, 17
Darth Vader 20, 31
Death Star 28, 31
Emperor 20, 31
Fett, Jango 8, 17
Jedi 5, 7, 18

Kenobi, Obi-Wan 6, 7
Leia, Princess 24
Palpatine 18, 19, 20
Rebel Alliance 24, 31
Skywalker, Luke 27, 31
Solo, Han 27
speeder bikes 14–15
starfighters 16
stormtroopers 20, 22, 26
Yoda 10

📖 READERS

My name is

_____

I have read this book ✔

Date

_____